Zoo Vets

Pamela Rushby

Contents

Zoo Vets

What Are Zoo Vets?

A vet is someone who has been trained to look after animals when they are sick or injured.

Some vets look after pets, such as cats, dogs and rabbits. Other vets look after farm animals, such as cows, horses and sheep. And other vets look after animals that live in zoos or wildlife parks, such as elephants, crocodiles, lions, monkeys, tortoises, lizards, bats and many more. These vets are called zoo vets.

A zoo vet checks the health of an elephant.

Zoo vets are specially trained to work with animals in zoos. They try to keep the animals healthy, and they treat them when the animals are sick or hurt.

A zoo vet takes care of a leopard cub.

In most zoos, animals live in large **enclosures**. There are plants, trees, rocks and pools in the enclosures that are similar to the animal's natural **habitat**. Some zoos have large open **ranges**, where animals can roam freely.

These rhinoceroses can roam freely in this open-range zoo.

Some zoos keep mostly one kind of animal, such as koalas or tigers. Other zoos breed **endangered** animals, so they will not become extinct.

Zoo vets work in all these kinds of zoos.

Vets care for an endangered tiger that has been rescued, before it is transported to a zoo.

What Zoo Vets Do

The biggest part of a zoo vet's job is keeping the animals in the zoo healthy. The vets check the animals every day for any signs of illness. Treating a sick animal quickly can stop diseases from spreading among the animals.

Sometimes, zoo vets do **research** about animals in the zoo. They might try to find out how fast a cheetah can *really* run, or what the best food is for a rare bird, such as a bird of paradise from Papua New Guinea. This knowledge is shared with other zoos. It helps scientists and vets to understand more about the animals.

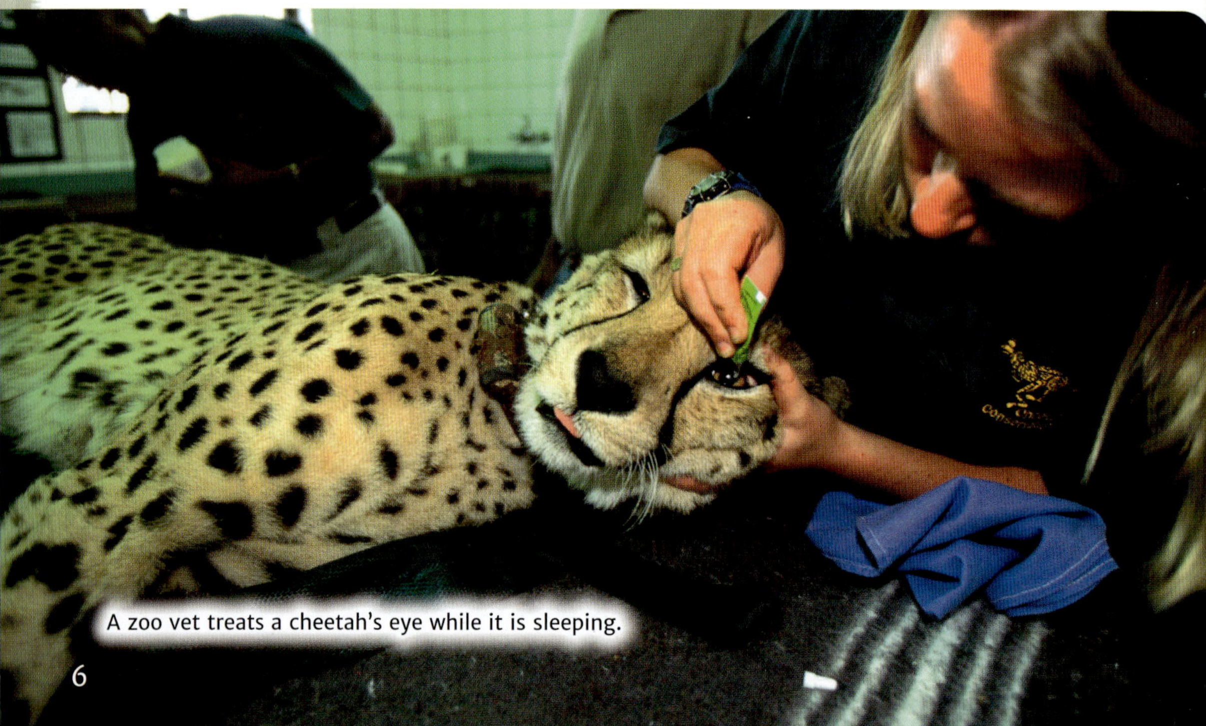

A zoo vet treats a cheetah's eye while it is sleeping.

Moving Animals

Zoos sometimes swap, or exchange, animals for breeding. A zoo with two female animals might swap one with a zoo that has two male animals of the same **species**. Then the animals may **breed**.

A pair of hippos enjoy the water together in their enclosure.

Kamili's Journey

When an animal is moved from one zoo to another, zoo vets have to plan the journey to make sure the animal is safe as it travels.

In 2019, a giraffe named Kamili was sent on a journey of 5834 kilometres from Perth Zoo in Western Australia to Orana Wildlife Park in New Zealand, as part of a breeding program. The zoo vets planned the trip carefully. They built a special travelling box and trained Kamili to be comfortable moving in and out of it. They checked the roads along the **route** to make sure there were no low bridges or powerlines that the travelling box would not fit under.

Kamili lived at Perth Zoo before her journey to New Zealand.

This is Kamili in her travelling box on her way to Orana Wildlife Park.

For part of the journey, Kamili travelled on a ship across the Tasman Sea. The zoo vets chose to move Kamili at a time of year when they knew the sea would be calm.

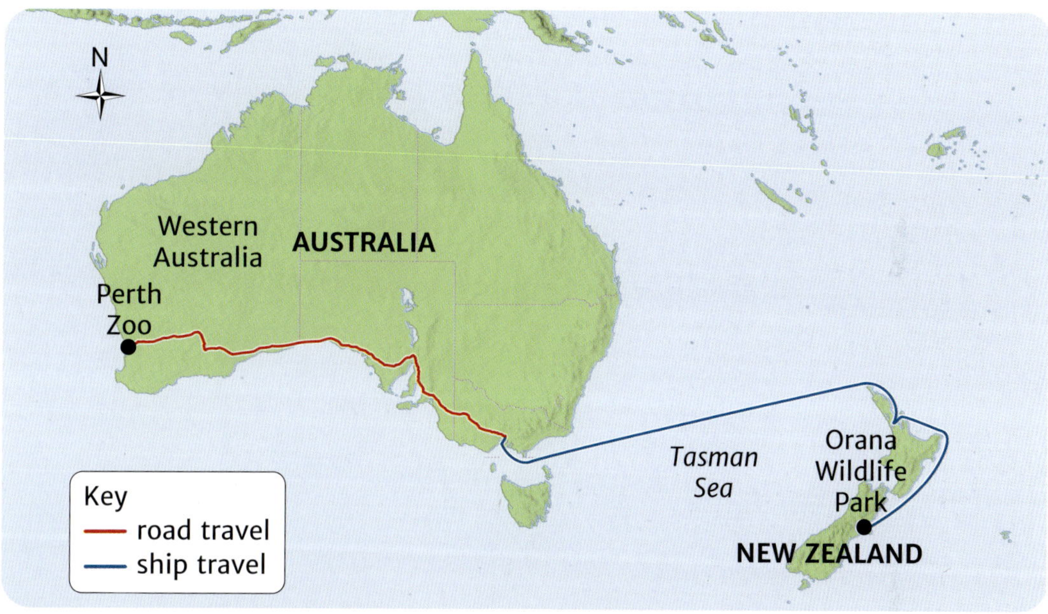

This map shows Kamili's journey by road and ship from Perth Zoo in Australia to Orana Wildlife Park in New Zealand.

A zoo vet travelled with Kamili to her new home. This was to make sure she was comfortable and eating well on the journey, and to report on her health to the vet at Orana Wildlife Park in New Zealand.

The journey was a success and Kamili settled in at her new home.

An Interview with a Zoo Vet

Zoo vet Dr Galit Tzipori works at a zoo that has many Australian animals. Here, Galit talks about the work she does every day.

What is your typical day like?

Every day is different.

Usually, I start by checking my notes from the day before. The notes tell me which animals need treatments and which animals need to be checked to see if they are improving.

Sometimes, **animal keepers** meet with me to report an injury or unusual behaviour. Then, we will go together to check on that animal.

On some days, I might have to deal with emergencies – for example, when injured wild animals are brought to the zoo.

Galit listens to a snake's heartbeat at her zoo.

What kinds of things does a zoo vet do?

Zoo vets do lots of different things to look after the health of the animals. I take blood from the animals for testing. I check their teeth. I do X-rays and medical checks.

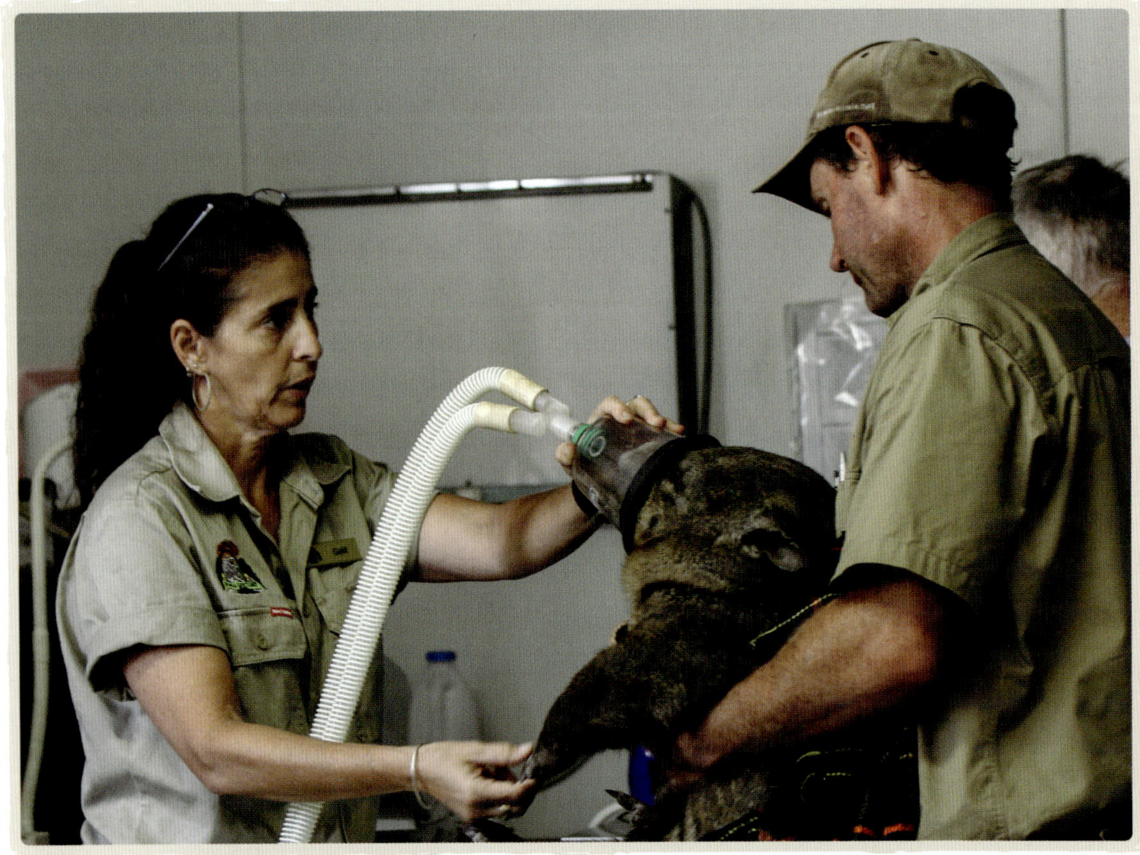

Some animals have to be given special medicine or gas to make them sleep before they can be safely moved, checked or treated.

Being a zoo vet is a problem-solving job. I work with Australian animals, but vets in other zoos around the world might care for more than 2000 different animals. These vets could be **operating** on a tiny lizard one day, and checking a 5000-kilogram elephant the next.

A zoo vet checks inside an elephant's mouth while two animal keepers help.

What is challenging about being a zoo vet?

A big problem for zoo vets is that the animals cannot tell us how they are feeling. For example, what might be the problem if a frog is not eating its food? Why has a peregrine falcon started limping? Vets have to look for what is causing the animal to be sick.

This 10-week-old panda is being checked by a zoo vet.

Once, one of my keepers reported a koala with a very runny nose. Tests showed this was not caused by a cold. What could it be? I ordered a **scan** of the koala's head. The scan showed the problem was a bad tooth. When the tooth was removed, the koala began to feel better.

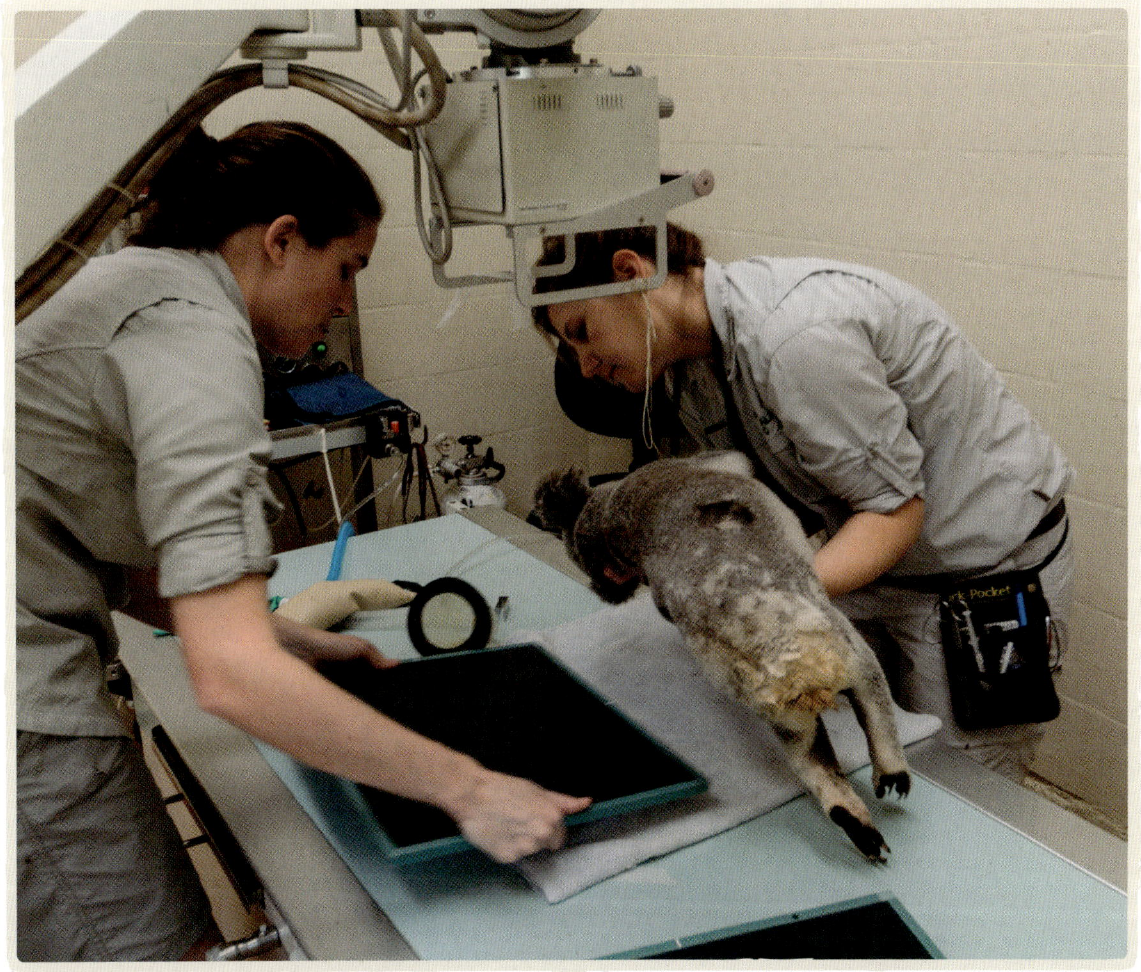

This koala is about to get an X-ray.

Can you tell us about a time when you were very worried about an animal?

We had a koala that was old and sick – and she had just had a joey. I was afraid the two-day-old joey would not survive. I decided to try and give the joey to another mother koala to look after. The joey was very small – it looked just like a little pink jellybean. It was not easy to take the joey from its mother's pouch and put it in the pouch of another female koala. Everyone at the zoo was delighted when the move went well. The joey, named Hermit, is now healthy and active, and almost two years old.

A baby koala is called a joey.

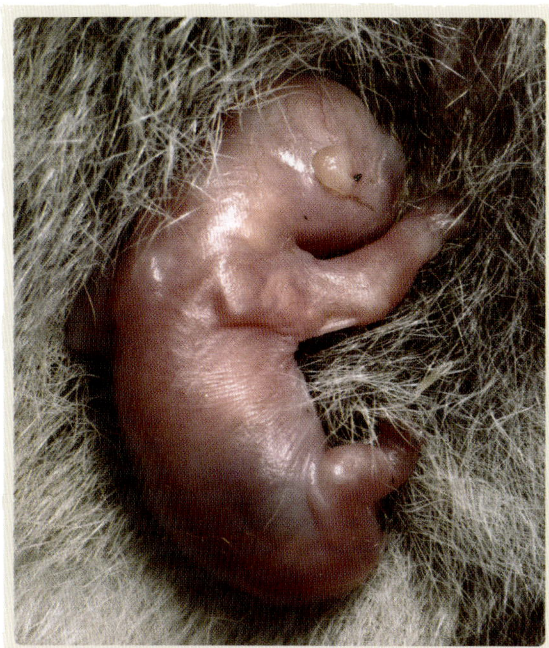

This koala joey is safe in the pouch.

Galit checks Hermit's heartbeat.

What is the best thing about being a zoo vet?

It is wonderful to have so many different animals to care for. You do have to be comfortable handling them all – from snakes to very large kangaroos and crocodiles. It is very **rewarding** to work with an animal over its whole life. I check that it is healthy when it is born, and I watch it grow and perhaps have babies of its own. Then I care for it as it grows old.

Zoo vets and animal keepers work together to check a python.

Some zoos help to breed endangered animals and then release them into the wild. Animals such as the Arabian oryx and Amur (say: *A-moo-r*) leopard have been saved from extinction in this way.

Arabian oryx

Amur leopard

How do you become a zoo vet?

People who love animals and want to become zoo vets usually study at **university**. Then, they might do work experience, or volunteer at a zoo to learn more about **exotic** species.

Becoming a zoo vet takes a lot of time and hard work.

Some zoos have junior animal-keeper programs, where children who are interested in animals visit a zoo for a day and learn about working there. Junior animal keepers might clean enclosures, prepare food and hand-feed – or even handle – some animals. It's a great way to find out more about what it is like to be a zoo vet.

This animal keeper is showing a student how to safely handle a baby alligator.

A Special Job

Zoo vets need to know a lot about many different kinds of animals. They keep the animals in zoos healthy. They stay in touch with other zoos, to share new knowledge. They also teach people who visit zoos about animals, and how important it is that animals are protected, so they will survive into the future.

Zoo vets do a very special job.

A zoo vet checks some ruffed lemurs.

Glossary

animal keepers (*noun*) people who work in zoos, feeding and caring for animals

breed (*verb*) to produce babies

enclosures (*noun*) fenced areas for animals

endangered (*adjective*) at risk of becoming extinct

exotic (*adjective*) from a different place

habitat (*noun*) the place where animals usually live

operating (*verb*) treating by surgery

ranges (*noun*) wide open spaces for animals

research (*noun*) a search for information, sometimes by doing experiments

rewarding (*adjective*) satisfying to do

route (*noun*) a path or set of paths to travel along

scan (*noun*) a test that looks inside the body using a machine

species (*noun*)	different types of plants or animals
university (*noun*)	a place to study after high school

Index